ROBOT CITY'S TOP PRIVATE DETECTIVE AGENCY,

ROBOT CITY CONFIDENTIAL INVESTIGATIONS,

IS ABOUT TO TAKE ON ITS TOUGHEST JOB YET!

MORNING, ROBOT CITY.
POPULATION: 15 MILLION HUMANS,
1 MILLION ROBOTS.

UNTIL RECENTLY, IT SEEMED LIKE WE DID A LOT OF THINKING AND NOT SO MUCH WORK.

ON THIS PARTICULAR DAY WE WERE BOTH DEEP IN THOUGHT. THEN *SHE* WALKED IN.

ROSIE MCFARLANE!

ONE OF THE FAMOUS ROBOT CITY AUTOMETTES!

I WAS HER BIGGEST FAN! ACTUALLY, THAT COAST-GUARD GUY CURTIS LIKED HER TOO, AND HE'S 300 FEET TALL, SO I GUESS THAT TECHNICALLY *HE* WAS HER BIGGEST FAN.

BUT I WAS HER *BEST* FAN-- FOR SURE! ROSIE AND LOLA CRUZ WERE MY ALL-TIME FAVORITE AUTOMETTES, BUT LOLA HAD LEFT THE TROUPE THE PREVIOUS YEAR, SO NOW ROSIE WAS THE ONLY GIRL FOR ME.

HEY, TAKE THE WEIGHT OFF THOSE SHINY LONG LEGS. ROD, GET THE LADY A CHAIR.

ROD--DID I MENTION THAT'S ME? MY FULL NAME IS RODNEY MARK II. I COULDN'T DECIDE WHICH NAME WAS BEST FOR A PRIVATE DETECTIVE, RODNEY OR MARK, SO I CHOSE BOTH. MIKE TOLD ME TO SHORTEN IT TO ROD--

ROD! SNAP OUT OF IT AND FIND THAT CHAIR. NOW, HOW CAN WE BE OF SERVICE TO YOU, MISS . . . ?

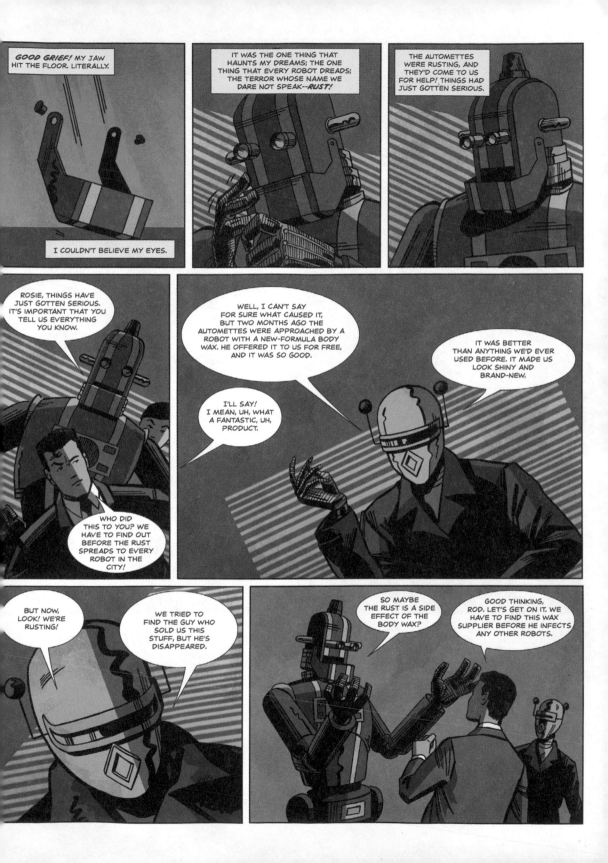

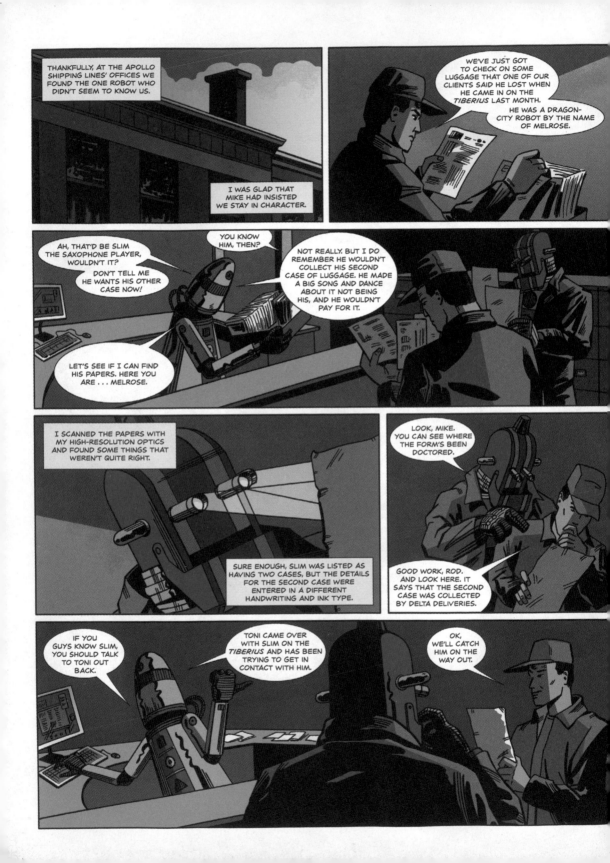

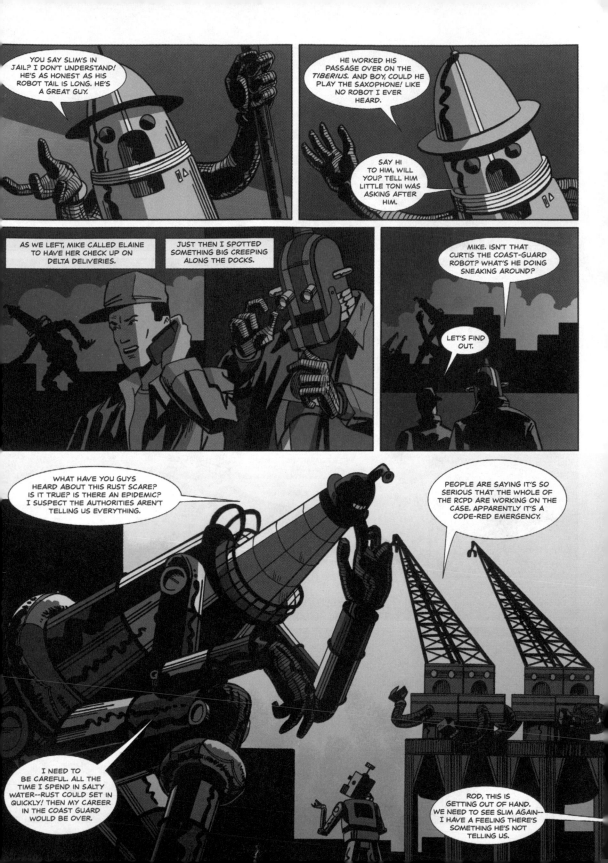

ROBOT CITY CENTRAL STATION. BUILT IN 1882 ON THE SITE OF THE OLD COTTON MARKET, IT'S GROWN UP WITH THE CITY. THEY'RE ALWAYS FILMING SOMETHING HERE.
WE LOCATED THE LUGGAGE LOCKERS ON THE WESTERN SIDE, BY THE SUBURBAN LINE PLATFORMS.
THERE THEY ARE.

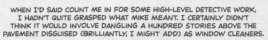

WHEN I'D SAID COUNT ME IN FOR SOME HIGH-LEVEL DETECTIVE WORK, I HADN'T QUITE GRASPED WHAT MIKE MEANT. I CERTAINLY DIDN'T THINK IT WOULD INVOLVE DANGLING A HUNDRED STORIES ABOVE THE PAVEMENT DISGUISED (BRILLIANTLY, I MIGHT ADD) AS WINDOW CLEANERS.

BECAUSE WE'RE A CONFIDENTIAL AGENCY, WE COULDN'T BOAST ABOUT HOW WE'D SAVED THE CITY FROM A RUST EPIDEMIC.

BUT LIEUTENANT COLE LET A FEW PEOPLE IN KEY PLACES KNOW WHO'D DONE WHAT, AND THE PHONE IN OUR OFFICE STARTED RINGING A BIT MORE.

WE STILL LIKE TO GET A LOT OF THINKING DONE, BUT I'VE STARTED GETTING UP EARLIER. LIKE, IN THE ACTUAL MORNING.

MIKE SAID THAT WE SHOULD HAVE A NIGHT OUT TO CELEBRATE, SO THAT'S US IN THE AUDIENCE. THAT'S MIKE AND HIS GIRL. YES, IT'S ELAINE--WHO'D HAVE THOUGHT?

AND THAT'S ME ALL DRESSED UP. MY GIRL'S NOT SITTING NEXT TO ME, BUT SHE IS HERE. . . . THIS IS HER BIG NUMBER COMING UP!

THE AUTOMETTES PUT TO REST ANY RUMORS ABOUT THEIR CONDITION WITH A SENSATIONAL NEW SHOW.

EVERYONE WAS WORRIED THAT AFTER HAVING TAKEN A LONG BREAK FROM PERFORMING THEY MIGHT BE A LITTLE BIT--YOU KNOW--*RUSTY!* BUT THEY'D BEEN REHEARSING. THEY WERE OUT OF THIS WORLD.

THE END